Beautiful
Me ©

Written by Rachel Saar
Illustrated by Jack Golden

Rachel Saar 2021

This book is dedicated to every child who wants to see themselves portrayed in a storybook, to my parents for raising me in a biracial home filled with love and acceptance, and to my loving husband and children who encouraged me to pursue this dream.

-Rachel Saar

My hair is kinky, curly in bright hues of orange and red.

My skin is a lovely carmel color.
It's soft and pretty on me.

My Mommy says it's a special gift from my birth country!

My eyes are green
like emeralds.
They shine wonderfully
clear and bright.

My Mommy says she gave me that hair,
as she hugs me with all her might!

My Skin is pale like fallen snow. It's as white as white can be.

My eyes are pretty and shiny.
They help me explore and see.

My hair is golden and long.
It shines like the morning sun.

MARS

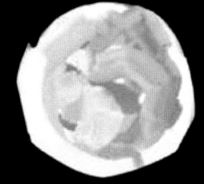
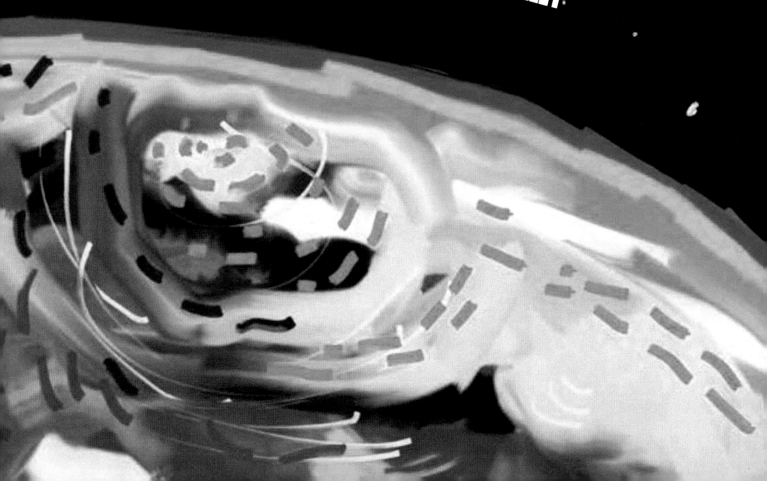

Where are you from?

Every human is beautiful and special, you and everyone!

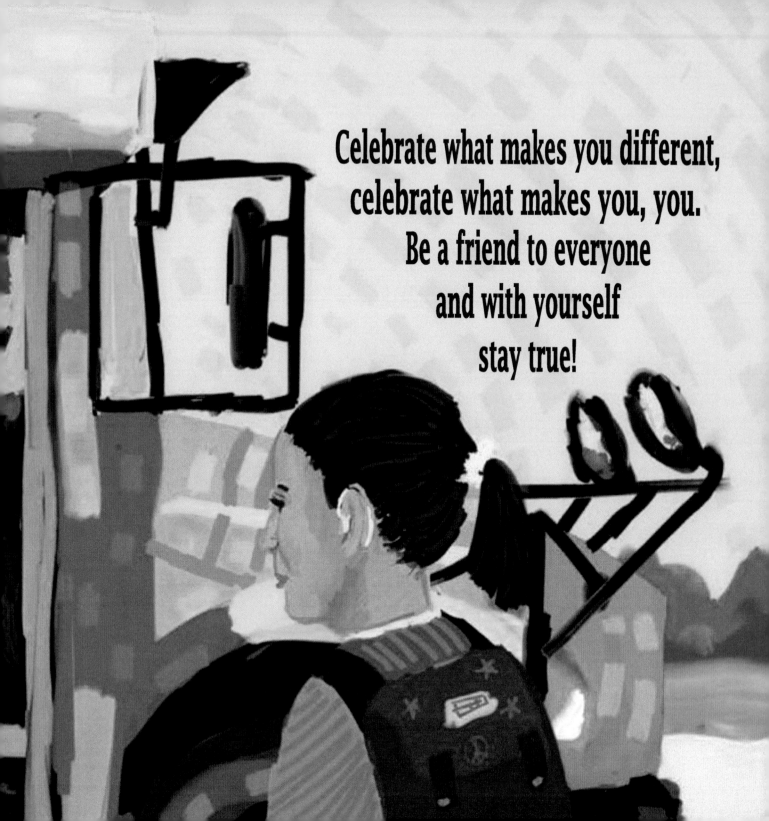

Celebrate what makes you different,
celebrate what makes you, you.
Be a friend to everyone
and with yourself
stay true!

About the Author

As a biracial child who did not look biracial, Rachel grew up never seeing pictures of families like her own in books. She loves seeing blended families and beautiful children of all races and ethnicities. Rachel's desire for all children to embrace the beauty in their families inspired her to write her first book, *Beautiful Me*. Rachel has always  enjoyed being creative and producing art. She particularly enjoys painting and writing. When thinking about writing children's books, Rachel wanted books that inspire, empower, intrigue, spark curiosity, promote acceptance, and provide beautiful art. She wanted books that encouraged children to be proud of their skin, their family, their hair, their size, their wonderful uniqueness. Rachel holds a Bachelor's degree in Liberal Arts from Marshall University. She has worked as a Social Worker in multiple settings, owned and operated her own boutique children's party business, worked in her family-owned Forensic Psychology practice, and currently does substitute teaching as well as travel planning. She believes it is never too late to follow your dreams. Rachel enjoys time with her husband and is most proud of being a Mom to four amazing children.

About the Illustrator

Jack Golden is an artist from Orange County, New York. *Beautiful Me* is the first children's book he has illustrated. Currently, Jack is studying psychology and studio art at the University of Scranton. In his free time, Jack enjoys going on hikes with his family, watching stand-up comedy, and playing with his wild dog, Obi. You can find more of his artwork on Instagram @jackgolden_art.

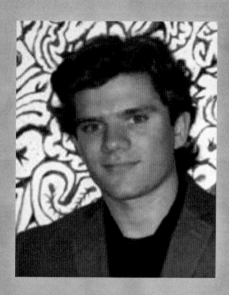

Made in the USA
Columbia, SC
07 February 2021